Capsized

Capsized

Anne Tews Schwab

P*

POLARIS PUBLICATIONS
An imprint of NORTH STAR PRESS OF ST. CLOUD, INC.
St. Cloud, Minnesota

Author photo © Andy King
http://www.akingphoto.com

Cover photo © Pat Dunsworth, White Bear Yacht Club;
www.patdunsworth.printroom.com

ISBN: 978-0-87839-706-8

Printed in the United States of America.

Published by Polaris Publications,
an imprint of North Star Press of St. Cloud, Inc.
P.O. Box 451
St. Cloud, MN 56302

www.northstarpress.com

For Christian, Jorie, JD, Reggie and Louie

Thank you to everyone in my large and loyal crew . . .
Mom and Dad
Jennifer and SallyJean
Amy
Katie
Tracee
Gale
Bonnie-Sue
Mellissa and Jyoti
Carrie
Kelly, Claire, Marsha, Anne, Ron, Mary and Mary
Hamline MFAC

Dani's story would have capsized without the support of all of you.

Happy Sailing!

MUSIC OVER WINDY LAKE
Green blue lake weeds clump/
Sailboats slip, tip. Far away/
one piano plays.

Contents

PROLOGUE—A LETTER TO UNCLE NOAH

Dear Uncle Noah,

I know you don't like
poetry—too many rules—
even haiku.

You know I don't like
to talk about me. But you
asked, and so I will.

I'll tell, but you'll have
to deal with the poetry.
Sorry. I need it.

Sometimes the only
way to tell the truth is by
following the rules.

Or at least know what rules to break.

So OK, no more quadruple haikus.
No more funky forms.
Just words set free,
        for you,
                from me.

Poetry? Yeah, but easy to read,
like rock n roll lyrics,
set to a solid backbeat.

So settle into your new chrome wheeled chair
        (are you getting used to it yet?)
spin the dial on your triple turntable
        (is Gamma still turning it down all the time?)
and rock to the rhythm of my super long story.

Keep getting better—
keep thinking positive—
keep trying to move your arms, your legs.

xoxo,
Dani

IN THE BEGINNING

Once upon a time
there was a little girl
with a mess of mud black curls
who loved to sail on Black Bear Lake.

For five years she giggled
on boats with Mama and Daddy
until that purple green sky day . . .

The wind came up, the boat went over,
Dani was trapped, between sail and cold water.

Daddy pulled her out, Mama dried her off,
Uncle Noah whisper sang her down -
even baby brother Will sang along.

But all the songs couldn't stop
       Dani's swamping tipping fear.
All the songs couldn't make
       her sailing love reappear.

After that, she wanted off the water.
But Daddy said all Biddles sailed;
Daddy said she had to sail forever.

Dani begged to stick to piano,
Daddy wouldn't listen to a single note.

Until . . .

Uncle Noah fell.
From a tall ship crow's nest.
Hit the deck, broke his neck, almost died.
       Even Daddy cried.

And in those foggy days of After,
Daddy agreed to a deal.
Dani could trade - piano for water -
after one last sailing weekend with Will.

A good plan
A fine plan
A perfect plan
Until the boys and the beers came in. . . .

THE BEGINNING OF THE END

The stage is set,
the story is ready,
let the races begin . . .

INCOMING

Doom shadows straightline
  across white-capped waves,
    as the blast of wind
      slaps the sails of our boat.

I hang on tight and shout.
  "Don't let us tip!"
    But the blast
      rams the words
        down my throat,
          and all that comes out
            is one long scream.

The mainsail snaps, the jib cracks,
  the boom swings and smacks,
    and almost knocks me out.

"Dani." Will's voice is calm and quiet.
  "Pop the jib and hike."
    For once in my life,
      I do what little brother says.

Hang on,
  hook my feet,
    lean back,
      hike.

No matter what Daddy says—these hands weren't meant for sailing.

FRENEMIES

"Starboard!" Will shouts,
    as my ex-best friend Mary,
        crash-smashes her boat through the waves
      all around us.

        Will jerks the tiller,
      hauls the main sheet,
      and we miss Typhoon Mary's port-tacking beast
by less than the width of a rope.

But his haul-dip-duck move
    jerks our boat up, up, up,
        and we tilt higher, higher, higher.

        I squeeze my eyes shut,
           sure we're about to go

              over.

freeze frame

dead air

silence

. . .

to tip

or splash down

that is

the question

PANIC ATTACK

White knuckling the boat edge,
      I prepare for disaster.
           Sure we're about to tip over.
      But Will stays calm, confident, quiet.
"You can let go. It's just a puff."

Easy for him to say.
      I know what a freak gust
          like this can do
      to a little sailboat
on a big lake.

I know all about
      getting thrown off
          getting trapped
              under a wicked white sail,
          getting shoved
      down into tar black

                  silence.

Just a puff?

      I don't think so.

I hunch into my lifejacket,
      anchor my feet in the hiking strap,
          hang on tight, tight, and
              pray, pray, pray.

PLEASE GOD, HEAR MY SONG

Please please pretty please,
don't let me slip,
don't let me slide out,
don't let me splash down
don't let me go deep
in the abyss
of the tangled cold dark lake.

Please, God,
make this wind stop.

BOUY ROUNDING

Sure enough, Will's right—we don't tip over.

The sailboat splash smacks
flat down on the water,
but I barely have a chance to exhale
before it's time to go around
the first buoy.

"Get the pole up, D!"
"I am, Captain Ahab!"

Behind us the rest of the X boat fleet
battles for buoy position.

"Room!"
"No room!"
"Rights!
"No rights!"

When do I get the right
to quit doing this,
to say no to sailing
forever?
To stay home with sweet Bessie,
my mellow, mahogany, upright piano?

According to Daddy?
Never.

I climb up on the deck,
shove the whisker pole in the mast,
try not to fall out while gust after evil gust
conspires to dump me.
Daddy makes me crew for Will because I'm a whole foot shorter
but I know the evil, awful wind can still swoosh up and get me.

When will Daddy get it?
I don't belong here.

My ponytail whips
into my eyes,
blurring the way
back to shore.

HYMN

My iPod is skipping,
my ear buds are soaking,
the wind has blasted
poor Beethoven away.

But my fingers remember,
his melody, his rhythms,
and I mash them
with a cool jazz
walking bass line.

I think of it as a hymn,
play the boat deck like a keyboard,
while singing the words in my head -

> *Christ, have mercy.*
> *Wind, have mercy.*
> *Black Bear Lake, have mercy on me.*
>
> *Please, God, don't me let fall out,*
> *even better, God, please make it stop,*
> *Please, blow the brutal wind*
> *far*
>   *far*
>   *away.*

GOD IS NOT A GOOD LISTENER

The wind zings,
    the boat tilts,
        the sails crack,
            and I slip.

Scrabbling for a hand hold,
    missing all the lines,
        crashing,
            banging,
                I go slamming straight down.
Past the white sail,
    over the slippery side,
        trying to stay on board,
            failing.

Here we go again -
    I'm falling,
        falling,
            falling,

                        going
                        down
                        down
                        down

                        Going
                        straight
                        down.

Except -
        This time I've got my lifejacket on
        This time the sail isn't shoving me under
        This time isn't like the first time.

        Thank you, God.

THE FIRST TIME

I was five.
I was trapped.
I was almost dead before
      Daddy pulled me out,
      dried me off,
      patted my shaking wet head.

His tree trunk arms wrapped me,
his yellow gold mustache smiled at me,
but nothing made me stop crying.

Before that day,
Daddy took me out for every race.
Before that day,
I loved it.
But that was all
      before.

After that day,
I never loved it again.

POP UP

I learned my lesson
       when I was five,
Wore a lifejacket
       ever since.

And now, my life jacket
       does its thing,
pops me right back up,
       brings me right back to fresh air.

Daddy motors up next to us,
       big and yellow in the tiny silver tin motorboat.
"Daddy, pull me out,
       Daddy, please?"

Daddy's blond-grey mustache quivers
       as he idles the motor,
reaches over and pulls me
       on board.

"Can we go in now?"
       I pretzel my arms
around my lifejacket-puffed chest.
       Daddy puts the motor in gear.

"You do know,"
       Daddy says,
"If this was a race,
       you'd have to get back on the sailboat."

I nod as he reaches
       behind him to grab
a thin fishy grey
       dry towel.

BULLSEYE

Daddy points a finger at my face.

"Remember tomorrow,
when the races begin, you
have to hang on, you have to stay in.
The deal was you sail the whole weekend with Will,
the deal was you help him win. If you
fall out, he loses the race. If
you fall out, the
deal is off."

Bullseye.

THE DEAL

"But Daddy, what if
    I fall in again?
        Can't Will get someone else
            to crew for him this weekend?"

I open my eyes
    ice-cream-sundae-with-a-cherry-on-top innocent.

Too bad Daddy is
    lactose intolerant.

"You're sailing
    with Will.
        There's no one else available.

And if you want to keep
    that old piano,
        you'll do it without complaining."

"I will, I promise,
    and after this weekend,
        I can stop sailing forever, right?"

"A Biddle
    never
        stops sailing."

THE BIDDLE CREED

I know the family creed,
      the evil tune haunts me awake and asleep.

Daddy sings it again anyway.

     A Biddle's a sailor,
     A Biddle is strong,
     The first Biddles were whalers,
     and this is their song.

I know the lyrics,
I know the rhythm,
I know the deal:
     I'm a Biddle,
     I'm doomed to sail.

I've heard this song
     twelve zillion times,
an endless loop
     that goes on and on

I've been hearing it forever,
     or at least since I was little,
since that awful day,
     that trapped-under-the-big-sail,
     lost-in-white-dead-silence,
     thinking-I-would-drown-for-sure,
nightmare day.

I WAS ONLY FIVE

I was only five
when the wind blasted,
and our boat flipped,
and I splash-crashed
into the water.

Caught under
the heavy white mainsail,
I clawed, kicked, fought, choked,
and by the time Daddy
dragged me,

out from under
the white-death sail coffin,
back into the righted but waterlogged boat,
I was shake-shivering through
my very first panic attack.

Mama wrapped me in thin arms,
she and Uncle Noah sang me down,
in harmonies that carried me
back into calm.
Daddy sailed on.

Maybe he felt bad, like Mama said he did,
but he made me finish that race that day.
He made me keep sailing,
again and again.
Every summer, every weekend, Daddy still made me sail.

Will tried to help, found different crews,
but Daddy said no, your sister sails with you.
Daddy said I'd get over it. Daddy said I'd learn to love it,
but it's been ten years now,
and his words still aren't true.

Will he ever stop pushing?

RUNAWAY

I'm wishing I was off the water,
playing piano inside,
instead of here shivering,
     in this fishy thin grey towel.

Daddy's landing the motorboat
at the end of the dock.
Mom is catching the bow.
     "Oh no, what happened, is everyone OK?"

Her pink sunburned nose is quivering,
her black binoculars swinging
loose around her Wonderland-
     Alice long neck.

Before I can answer,
Will's landing the sailboat,
jumping onto the dock,
     tying up.

He's pulling off a hiking boot,
dumping water back into the lake,
telling Mom what happened.
     "Dani fell in."

Mom is trying to hug me,
but I'm ducking away,
dropping my towel,
     just wanting to get inside.

Daddy is telling me
to help Will with the sailboat,
Daddy is saying,
     "You know the rules. Stay."

I'm the rule follower,
not the rule breaker,
but this time I dare to say
     "No."

Daddy's shock is turning him
pumpkin orange.
Fairy Godmother Mom is rescuing me.
     "Ed, let her go."

ESCAPE

I run up the beach,
      across the lawn,
           towards the house,
                slip sliding straight
                     for the back door.

Wet hair slapping,
      wet pants sucking,
           wet t-shirt sticking
                in all the wrong places.
                     I pray no one sees me.

I just want to get inside -
      to dry land,
           to safety.
                I just want to get to my happy place,
                my piano,
                     my Bessie.

LOCKED OUT

"What the—?"
      I twist
      turn
      slap the silver knob.
"We never lock this door!"

"DD?"
      A familiar voice
      rumbles
      from the front of the house.
"Yo? You back there?"

"Mike!"
      I give the door a last
      kick
      and run around to the driveway next door.
"I missed you so much! When did you get home? Whoa—what happened to your head?"

"Shaved it."
      Mike's forever sticking up
      black clumps of hair
      are gone, mowed down to scalp stubble.
"Juvie sucks."
      He smacks the side of
      of his up-on-blocks
      gold Mustang.
"And this thing still don't work."

"You look—"
      I open my arms,
      but his weed green eyes slip,
      and his grease spattered hands flick
      me away from his chest.
"—different."

"You look—"
      He watches me back off
      as he leans on the open hood,
      and the look on his indoor pale face
      makes me shiver.
"—wet."

DEAD WHITE DUDES

Mike points his wrench
at the earbuds dripping
down around my neck.
     "Still rockin with the guys in the wigs?"

I make a face.
"Stupid lake killed my iPod."

     "Again? This time you gonna reload with some decent flow?"

"Better than Beethoven and Bach?
I don't think so."

     I twist the cords
     and tuck the fried buds
     back in my pocket.
"They're better than whatever this is."
     I wave a hand
     at the pounding flood of
     what Daddy would call
        word porn,
     screaming from the speakers
     on the hood of his car.

Mike snort-rolls his eyes
and I snort-roll mine back
and just for a second
     it feels like old times.

OLD TIMES

In the old days,
the good days,
Mike and I did everything together.

My daddy liked him then,
the boy who came over every day,
the boy who always had something funny to say.

We built tree-houses and forts,
we whipped snowballs at his brutal big brothers,
we snuck peanut butter cookies from the oven,
we rode our ten speeds around the park together.

And then his dad left.

After that, my daddy said
Mike was trouble,
but I knew Mike was still the same inside.

I knew Mike still needed an ally,
I knew Mike still needed a friend,
I knew Mike still needed me.

NEW SUBJECT

"You still have that Harley?"

      "Yeah. So?" For a fast second,
      his smile is old Mike style.
      Happy, relaxed, all for me.

"So you said you'd take me for a ride when you got back."

      "Your dad said no."

            I look across the yard to the lake.
            Daddy's still talking at Will.
            I lean in quick and grab Mike's hand.

"If we go now, Daddy won't even know."
I squeeze and smile and giggle.

      Old Mike would have laughed back,
      grabbed my waist,
      pulled me on his Harley.

      But this Mike—
      this new Mike—
      pushes me away.

      "Gimme a break—I just got outta Juvie, okay?"

"Danielle!" Daddy's voice cuts
      through the wind torn air.
         "Inside—
              Now!"

I whisper, "Should I sneak out later?"

      Mike shakes his head
      and turns away.

OLD MIKE/NEW MIKE

What's going on?

STAY AWAY FROM MIKE

Daddy frowns me
inside. "That boy is trouble."

I auto answer
with words I've spouted
a zillion,
      trillion,
           times.

"It wasn't his fault."

Daddy shakes his head
and a buoy red blistered finger.
"He should still be in Juvie."

"But it wasn't his fault!"

"He's a fighter.
He's bad news.
And you'll stay away
unless you want that piano
to go to charity."

"It wasn't his fault,"
I re-whisper,
but Daddy is gone—
he's not listening—
      again.

PLAY IT OUT

Fighting a tsunami of tears,
I straightline for the living room.
I need to play out
the humiliation and freak out,
the watery end of the day.

I splash down on her faded
oak-spindly bench.

I tuck my legs under
            and arch my fingers over
the ivory ebony
            keyboard,
while below me
            the bench warms,
and my tears
            turn to salt,
drying crusty and tight
            on the sides of my face.

I sink into the waves,
            of the music that rises,
                        from the black and white truth.
                                    My piano, my Bessie, is the one friend I can always count on.
                        The one friend who never changes.
            The one friend who's always safe
and always opens her arms to me.

BESSIE

She's old,
she's temperamental,
she's named after a black and white cow,
but she's always there for me.

For now.

Waiting for my fingers,
understanding my need
to play away,
my panic, rage, confusion.
Bessie lets me mix,
Mozart and the Grateful Dead,
Rachmaninoff and
the Rolling Stones.

How could Daddy be talking about giving her away?

I splash-bash
melody,
harmony,
rhythms together.

On faded ivories and chipped ebonies,
my left hand lays down *Yellow Submarine*,
while my right runs wild
with good old Shostakovich.
The swirling notes of
Dmitri's *Symphony
No. 5 in D Minor*
is frenzied and chaotic,
out of tune and out of breath,
spinning almost out of control,
before finally coming back
home.

Sharps,   flats,
      old,   older,
            ragtime,   blues,   jazz,   classical,
Elvis, Scott Joplin,
      Beatles, Jelly Roll Martin.
Dissonance and order,
      ragtime and romance,
            rock and classical,
                  straight and syncopation—
I mash up and the mash ups
soothe and smooth
nasty memories of wind
and water
and New/Old Mike's rejection.

STOP TIME

I play until Daddy stops me.

"Enough." He points at the clock.
"Time for dinner and bed.
You've got a big weekend ahead."

My fingers twitch,
Bessie's low notes ring,
but I know there's no point in a fight.

"Two races tomorrow,"
Daddy reminds me.
"Two more the day after that."

"I know how regattas work, Dad."

How could I forget?

A Biddle never stops sailing.

RACE DAY

The next morning,
the sun is barely cracking
through the corners of my curtains
when Mom bangs my bedroom door open,
and flicks on the too bright light.

"Get up, wake up, get out of bed, sleepyhead!"

"Five more minutes,"
        I mumble
                from under my comfy
                        cozy fluffy yellow pillow.
                                But Mom takes the pillow,
                        pats my rats-nest bedhead
                and chirps, "Time to get ready
        for the races!"

"Nooooo,"
        I moan.

                        Mom rubs my back.
                "If you get up now,
        I'll make you pancakes
with caramel syrup.
You'll need the energy today."

"Is it windy?"
                        "A little bit."
                Mom sounds
        apologetic.
"But not too bad.
Not yet. You should be OK."

I moan groan the pillow
        back over my face.
I want
        to stay in bed
                forever

                        or at least for
five . . .
        more . . .
                minutes . . .

COUNTDOWN

"Danielle! Time to go!"

"Yikes!"

Clothes,
     teeth,
          hair.

Downstairs
     through the kitchen dash,
          Flight of the Bumblebee fast.

Snatch a Pop Tart
     from Daddy's surprised hand,
          as he talks doctor stuff
               on his cell phone,

          kiss Mom's
               tea-scented cheek,

          grab my blue lifejacket
          and yell.
               "Let's go, Will!"

If Old Mike were out,
     he'd give me a shout,
          tell me something smart, like 'don't drown today,'
               but New Mike just jacks up
                    his old car and sticks his head in.

Will catches up,
     bouncing and hopping
          like an overgrown goldendoodle.
Nip, nip, yap, yelp, he sputters,
     "Where were you?
          You're late!
               I've been ready to go
                    forever!"
                         "Alarm didn't go off,"
                              I say around a mouthful
                                   of Pop Tart.

"Good luck, kids!"
     Mom's voice sails
          across the lawn.
               "Be careful!
                    Wear your lifejackets and—"
                         Daddy's shout cuts her off,
                              "Sail fast and hang on!"

31

TOWING TIME

With the sailboat tied up behind us,
        the old motorboat has to try harder.

        The 9.9 horsepower,
            neon blue motor,
                painted to deter motor-robbers,
                    grumbles as I rev it.
        A set of old, wooden,
            splintery emergency oars,
                ice jugs, sail bags, battens,
                    shake, rattle, clatter,
                        slipping with every wave we hit.

I wish I didn't have to
        drive this thing.

I wish Will was
        old enough to take a turn.

        Obviously Will
            wishes it too.

After all, Will thinks every boat is his castle—
        he's the crown prince,
            heir to Daddy's watery kingdom,
        while I'm just a scrawny grey dungeon rat
scurrying in the shadows
        desperate to stay away
from their water and wind.

"C'mon, D," the water prince prods me
        with his ridiculously long legs.
"Can't you get this thing
        to go any faster?
We gotta get
        to the Yacht Club to practice!"

LANDING

I cut the motor
when I see the boathouse.

Too late.

"Whoa!"
A foot catches our bow
an instant before
we smashcrash the dock.

A hand grabs the line
hanging off the front
of our boat.
"Want me to tie you up?"

Tan long fingers loop
a bowline around
the nearest dock post.

I pull my tongue back in my mouth.

Ice blue *(or are they sea green?)*
eyes that shine *(or do they shimmer?),*
from a magazine-perfect *(or is it art gallery handsome?)*
tanned face.
Chiseled chin,
sculpted cheekbones,
glossy skin that gleams,
like a concert grand piano.

"Will," I whisper hiss.
      "Who.
            Is.
                  That?"

Will's eyes slit.
      "Don't you recognize him?
      That's Iowa Sam.

      Comes to Minnesota once a year—
            just for this regatta.
      Every year, he wins.

      But not this year.

      This year is my year.

      This year I'm going to beat him."

This year, I'm in love.

SAM

Sam drops
>   a smile
>   down on me.

>   I flop
>   like a fish
>   caught
>   in a net.

"Are you Will's sister?"

I wave my hands,
>   flutter my lips,
>   yap
stupidly
>   back at him.

>   "Hi, yes,
sister, Will,
>   Dani, no,
>   I mean,
>   Danielle
>   is
>   name me."
>   An idiot
>   I am.

But Sam doesn't seem
>   to mind.

"Danielle, huh?
Nice name."
>   He kicks a dried piece
>   of goose poop into the water,
>   leans on the dock post,
>   keeps smiling.

SAM'S HAND

Sam's hand
is stretched
towards me.
Sam's hand
is waiting
to help me.
Sam's hand
is ready
to take me out of my silver tin carriage
before it turns back into a normal motorboat again.

"Oh! Thanks!"

I jump, stand, reach,
stretch for his hand
but before I can grab,
      the motorboat tilts
      and the lake swoops
      and weedy water splashes in.

DEAR GOD

Dear God,
please don't let me
   fall in.
Not now,
Not here,
I'll do
   anything,
   anything,
   anything . . .

SAVIOR SAM

Strong arms
      strong hands
strong Sam
      saves me.

Good-bye,
      Lake Hell,
Hello,
      Sam Heaven.

I never thought I'd get an insta-crush
on a guy who is a sailor.
Most sailors are as annoying
as my big little brother,
but Sam is different,
I can tell,
Sam is perfect for me.

He's everything
that Mike isn't.

Short but solid,
with biceps that ripple
under a tight white t-shirt
and an above-the-waist red lifejacket.

A flop of nut-brown hair
sweeps over his left eye
he glides like a dancer,
his voice is like music,
like an opera singer,
like one of those famous three tenors.

I DIDN'T KNOW

"I didn't know."

"What?"

"That Will even had a sister."

>"Dani!"

"Is that Will?"

"No."

>"Dani, let's go!"

"Well, maybe."

"Do you have to go?"

"I guess so."

"Will I see you at the party?"

"What party?"

>"Dani—I'm gonna tell Dad!"

"The regatta party—after the races."

"Of course."

"Cool. Good luck out there today."

>"Dani!"

"You too."

SAILBOAT RACES AND OPERAS

Up and down,
　　　loud and soft,
melodramatic
　　　and full of
insults, threats and warnings.

Sailboat racing
　　　is a lot like
opera.

Shouts, whispers,
　　　curses, lullabies.
Strategy, story,
　　　costumes, scenery.
A frantic frenzy on
　　　a watery stage.

The audience sits
on pontoon boats and Jet Skis,
　　　instead of in red velvet seats.

The audience uses
high powered binoculars,
　　　instead of silver opera glasses,

The audience watches
sailors costumed in lifejackets,
　　　instead of in silk, cotton, velvet, and wool,

as they fight across cresting whitecaps,
with sails, strategy and swear words,
　　　instead of wooden swords and songs,

while on the backs of their vessels
names run like subtitles—
　　　"Cookie Monster,"
　　　"Mission From God,"
　　　"Auf Wiedersehen,"
　　　"Sayonara."

NORMALLY

Normally, I spend the whole race
     wishing I was somewhere,
                anywhere
       else.

              Checking my watch,
       doing a countdown,
     until I can get home
to Bessie.

But this time,
     I don't check the time.
         I hardly even think
            about Bessie.

         This time,
     I just watch
Sam.

RACE ONE

Will isn't a yeller,
but he yells at me today as I
keep track of Sam
but lose track of
the countdown to the start,
the other boats coming up on port tack,
the incoming puffs that shadow zing across the blue water.

I almost feel guilty,
when Will has to reach over
and grab the line out of my hand.

I almost feel bad, that I'm not trimming the jib properly.
I'm not lifting and dropping the board on time.
I'm not adjusting the outhaul, the downhaul.
But how can I do any of that,
when Sam is sailing so close behind us?

Sam comes close,
closer and closer,
but Will dodges and ducks
and covers and cuts,
and beats him to the finish line by three seconds.

RACE TWO

Race Two
is a lot like
Race One.

I watch Sam.
Will sails to win.
Sam comes in second
again.

Even though
Will's my brother,
and his boat is my boat too,
I kind of hope
that in the races tomorrow,
Sam pulls out at least one win.

REGATTA PARTIES—A TRUTHFUL HAIKU

Regatta parties.
Sailor brag fests. Ego-fueled
boring story times.

"See you at the party, Sam!"

HOME AGAIN HOME AGAIN

When Will and I get home,
Mike is working
on a disembodied engine,
laid out on the strip of dead grass
between our house and his.

He glances up
as we hit the dock,
and the look on his face
is a twist of Old and New.

But when I make a move
to go to him,
he grabs a wrench
and turns away.

I lift my head,
giraffe-neck high,
and walk right on past.

"C'mon, Will,"
I call to my turtle-slow brother.

"Let's go get ready
for the party.
I promised Sam
I'd see him there."

SURPRISING MOM

"Mom?"

I throw down my sailing gear and bang into the kitchen.
	"How much time do I have?

Mom wipes cookie dough off the corner of her mouth.
	"Until the cookies are done?"

	"Until the party!"
	"What party?"
	"The regatta party."
	"You're going?"
	"Of course!"

A scoop of dough slides
off the spoon in her hand
as she shakes her head,
scrunches her eyes,
repeats two more times,
	"You're going?"

JUST WHAT THE DOCTOR ORDERED

Still dressed in his scrubs,
Daddy charges into the kitchen.

"Can't believe
I had to go in today.
What did I miss?
How'd the races go?
What happened?
Where's Will?"

He scoops up raw cookie dough,
shoves it in his mouth.
"Did you stay in the boat?
Did Will do it?
Did he win?"

I make a face
at his puffed-out dough cheeks.
"I stayed in and
       we
won both races.
But Sam—Sam—
Sam was a super close second."

Daddy gulps a glass of milk,
drops the empty in the sink.
"Sam Fletcher?
The Iowa kid?
I thought he aged out last year."

"Little Sammy Junior is here?"
Mom's voice octaves up.
"I haven't seen his family in years!
Did his mom and dad come this time?"

IOWA BOY

"No idea." I shrug.

Before Mom can ask any more,
Will comes dripping inside.

Daddy spins and spews out questions.
"How close was he, that Iowa boy?
You've got to watch out for that one, Will."

"Yeah, but Dad, you shoulda seen how I covered his . . ."

Daddy shoots him a look,
and Will ducks a grin
as he pulls off
his wet hiking boots and keeps talking.
"I covered every tack, jibe,
read every shift, puff,
sailed so smooth
even Dani stayed on."

Will punches my shoulder.
I frown-rub and slide
out of reach.

"How did he get so close?" Daddy demands.

Will pulls off wet sailing pants,
strips down a pair of
blue plaid cotton boxers.

"Will," I groan,
look up and away.
Will's never heard of modesty.

"Crispy new sail," Will shrugs.
"Better boat speed.
Maybe if I had—"

Daddy cuts him off.
"Boat speed depends on the skipper."

"But a new sail wouldn't hurt."

Daddy frowns.

Will hurries on.
"Anyways,
we stayed in front,
pretty much the whole time,
he never had a chance—
right, D?"

"We can't let him
get that close tomorrow.
This is your year
to go undefeated."
Dad pulls out paper,
            pencils,
                        plastic boats.
"I'm still on call,
so in case I miss it,
let's figure out a battle plan now."
Time for us to talk strategy."

Time for me to go.

I slip-slide to the stove,
juggle a just-out-of-the-oven cookie,
scurry on up to my room to get ready.

FINALLY

"Kids, are you ready?"
      Daddy calls from the doorway.

"Your mother and I
      are waiting."

Finally, it's time
      for the party.

I dash across
      the driveway and wonder—

If Mike sees me in my
      little red tank top, will he notice?

I pretend not to look
      as I do a flyby.

I pretend not to see him
      working—
            on his shiny rusty up-on-blocks car.

      wearing—
            faded-in-all-the-right-places jeans,

      clanking—
            his tools in time to the beat box rap thudding

out from the speaker beside him.

DO YOU SEE WHAT I SEE?

Daddy drives, Mom rides shotgun,
Will jumps in the backseat
too close to me.

He folds his long legs,
bangs my ribs with his elbow,
jabs his chin at his window,
      at Mike.

"You talk to him yet?"

I point out the other side.

"Oh, look," I say,
"Mrs. McGruber had
her house painted blue this week."

SEARCH PARTY

I try to lose myself in the music,
but I can't hear it over the shouting contest,
of bragging, storytelling, teenage sailors.

I swear, if I have to listen to
another story about a shift and a lift and a puff,
I'm going to self-destruct.

I scoop up guac with toasted tortilla chips,
move across the thick white carpet,
search for the one sailor I want to see.

A swinging door leads into the next room,
and when I push through I find something
even better than Sam.

BLACK DIAMOND

Piano
Concert grand
Shining, elegant, stunning,
"Making no quality compromises"
Expecting, awaiting, promising,
Exquisite perfection—
Steinway

WOW!

If I play, will she answer?

I have to try.

My fingers drop and I
      melt
            into the keys.

Yellow rays of sweet salted music
      drift across the white room,
          lift like a prayer,
              ride the currents above
                  the sailor-scented air.

HEART AND SOUL

"You're good." Sam slides
on the slick bench next to me.

Goosebumps tingle
down my arms and
       zing
to my fingers that
      slip
           off
the keys.

"What was that?"
Sam's voice is honey-
cinnamon-sugar-toasty.
"Bach? Beethoven?"

"Mozart—
and the Beatles."

"The Beatles with Mozart?"

"I like to do mash ups."

Sam stretches his fingers
      over ten bone white keys.
"I took ten years of piano lessons.
      Check out my mash."

He drops his hands,
      attacks.

                        THUNK
                THUD
                       SMASH
I want to cover
      Steiny's keys and protect her,
            but Sam doesn't notice
                  as he shouts over the noise,
                        the awful, horrible, noise, noise, noise, noise.
      "C'mon,
            play along,
                I know
                    you know
                       this song!"

WHIRLING DERVISH

His fingers spin disaster faster than a F5 tornado as he Tasmanian devilizes
innocent ivories, killing my goosebumpy tingles and suddenly looking
a lot less amazing. I'm starting to wonder if Sam is the right
guy or if he's just another egotistical sailor.

Sam plays mistakes loud and louder,
laughs and repeats and bumps
my shoulder. "I can see why
you like this—it's easy,
no pressure." He whacks
Steiny's keys and I
barely hold back
from the urge
to shove his
hands off—
away.

GRIZZLY BEARS AND SALMON

"Dad! I Found Him!"

Will's shout stops
the painful Steiny attack.

"Young Sam Fletcher."
Daddy reaches for Sam's hand
and when he pulls Sam to stand
between him and Will,
Sam looks like a pink salmon
caught in the paws
of a pair of yellow blonde
oversized grizzly bears.

He's closer to my height,
probably a foot shorter,
than giant Daddy and Will,
but his arms are so strong,
and his back is so straight,
that he looks like he could fight them both.

Daddy hangs on
to Sam's hand as he growls,
"Tell me about your season.
Have you really won every race
back there in Iowa?"

THE SALMON TURNS INTO A FOX

Sam lets Daddy
keep his fisted grip,
but he's easy grinning,
ropey arms rippling,
as he gives Daddy a list
of his winnings.

The way he's spinning
his stories to Daddy,
reminds me of a red fox running,
carrying his fresh caught fish
away from the snapping beaks
of the hungry honking geese
that live on the shores of Black Bear Lake.

"It was that redhead girl," Sam says.
"Who almost won the second race for me."

Will spins and glares at me.
"That's your Mary."

      "She's not *my* Mary!"

"I don't think Mary meant to,"
      Sam cuts in.
"Actually, she port-tacked me.
      But by the time I realized
she wasn't going to tack away,
      it was too late.
I had to duck her
      and when I did,
I hit that lift."

"Mary," Will mutters.

"You got lucky." Dad releases
      Sam's hand, drops
a paw on Will's shoulder.
      "Come on, son,
let's go check the standings."

At the door
        they pause
to look back
        at me.

"Are you coming?"

I shake my head,
        no,
and off they go
and I brace myself for more
piano attack,
but Sam doesn't sit
on Steiny's warm bench.

He shields his eyes and asks,
"Is Mary here?"

MY FORMER BEST FRIEND, MARY

Mary and I
used to do
everything
          together.
First steps,
first dolls,
first music lessons too—
          we shared everything.
We sang
and danced
to music
          older than Elvis.
She'd sing
while I played
and we were a team—
          a duet.
We got big
on YouTube—
a thousand hit
          sensation

but then

Mary told me
I was the one
who everyone said
          had the talent.
Mary told me
I should just
go
          solo.
I said I couldn't
I wouldn't
I didn't
          want to do it alone,
but she drifted away,
off to the races,
off to the water,
          to the lake and the sun-toasted sailor boys

I still miss her stories,
I still miss her singing,
I almost even miss
        her giggles.

Sometimes
I can't help
but wonder—

        If I find
        a sailor boy of my own,
        will she sing with me
                again?

LOOKING FOR MARY

"She's here," I say.
I stand beside Sam,
close enough to smell him,
      inhale, exhale,
and point across the room.

"Right there," I say,
      "By the door.
      The one in the pink
      with the four Johnson boys."

HERE SHE COMES

When Mary sees us looking
she waves and hurries over
and squishes her giggly body
between us.

I fall back onto the piano bench,
as she spins towards Sam.

She wags a finger in his face,
like he's been naughty.

"That wasn't nice of you
to go off in that lift
and leave me behind with no wind!
If I'd stayed in the breeze,
I could have kept up,
heck, I think I could have even beaten
Dani and Will."

She hip checks me
and giggle wiggles.

YOU CAN'T BEAT US

"You can't beat us."

"Really?"
      Mary stares at me, those evil/innocent
      eyes wide as tide pools.
"Why not?"

"Because . . .
      because . . .
            just because."

"It's supposed to be
super windy tomorrow."

"Yeah? That'll be great!" Sam grins.

Mary shakes her head.
"Not for Dani."

I try to stop her,
try to push her away,
try to cut her off before she says what I know she's going to say.
"I'll be fine."

"But you're so scared
of windy days."
      Mary's voice is like a drippy Popsicle
      as she leans close
      and squeezes my shoulder.
"It would be just awful
if you had another one
of those scary panic attacks."
      Her whisper is louder than a shout,
      as her eyes slide between me and Sam,
      and her hand squeezes, squeezes, squeezes.

REDHEADS

Judas was a redhead

Mary is one too

UPSIDE DOWN AND DROWNING

"Mary!" I yelp.

Mary is doing
a hands-up, who-me?
back-away-smile thing.

Sam is looking at me
with pity wrinkles flickering
across his movie-star tan face.
"Not a fan of heavy wind, huh?"

Something is shifting
        in his voice
        in his eyes
and in my heart
I'm feeling like I'm five
        all over again.

"I had a bad experience once."

"But haven't you been sailing your whole life?
Didn't you grow up on the water?"

Sam is looking
        confused
and I am fighting
        a scream.

"You'd never understand."

Sam pats my back,
sweet soft as a new daddy
comforting a squalling squawking baby.
"Don't worry—you'll probably be OK—
I heard it's only supposed to blow
five to ten tomorrow."

"But just in case," Sam goes on,
"'I'll be sure to keep an eye on you."

His smile bonfires through me so bright
that I hardly notice Mary's chirpy bubble.
"Me too!"

I COULD TELL HIM

I could tell him—

how the blasts of wind sound
like the beating of a million
demon drum circles.

I could tell him—

how the slapping sails sound
like a symphony
from hell.

I could tell him—
but I don't.

I don't want
his sympathy.
I don't want
his empathy.
I don't want
his pity.

I just want
him
to want
me.

CHAUFFEUR

"Dani—we're leaving."
       Daddy's back,
but I'm not ready
       to leave the party
yet.

"Sir," Sam says,
       "I'd be happy
to drive Dani—
       and Mary too—
home tonight."

Daddy frowns,
       but Mom elbows
him into agreeing,
       and finally they leave,
towing Will behind.

Old fashioned as
       a black and white movie,
Sam wings
       his elbows out.
"Ladies?"

One for silent me—

One for jibber-jabbering Mary.

I wish Mary weren't
       with us.
I wish Mary wasn't
       so happy.
I wish Mary didn't make guys
       stop and stare.

I tell myself,
       It's fine,
          it's fine,
              everything's fine.

It's not like Sam's
       mine.
It's not like I own him.

THE DROP OFF

My house is closer,
  so it makes sense that Sam
    drops me off first.

Mary is in the car,
  so it makes sense that Sam
    talks to both of us.

It makes sense,
  but I don't want it to make sense.
    I just want Sam.

SHOTGUN

When I get out,
Mary follows me,
     up the driveway,
     away from the car,
     out range of Sam's ears.
Her whisper is warm and gaspy.

"I think he's perfect."

"For who?"

"For you, silly,
perfect for you!"

Mary giggle-hip-checks me,
     skip-run-jumps,
     back in the car,
into the front seat
close, too close,
to Sam.

MARY LOVES ME

Mary is my friend I know,
for she often tells me so,
I can trust her with this boy,
she won't steal my newfound joy.

Yes, I can trust her,
Yes, I can trust her,
Yes, I can trust her,

She often tells me so.

I'M NOT WORRIED

To the house,
to the door,
to Bessie, I go.

I play
pianissimo so I don't wake
anyone else
and I don't worry
about Sam and Mary
alone in the car.

I don't think
about them laughing.

I don't visualize
them sitting close to each other
in the front seat together.

I think
I'm doing just fine,
with my not-worrying,
not-thinking,
not-visualizing,
until I realize
I'm playing everything

in d minor.

the saddest key

d minor is
despair
worry
depression

d minor is
melodramatic
over the top

if old mike were here
he'd tell me to stop
playing everything in
d minor

BEDTIME

I'm changing into fuzzy jammies,
      wishing I could talk to Mike
      the way I always used to,
      when my wishing
      is interrupted
by my chirping cell.

I jump, I grab, I hope—
      could it be?

Could Old Mike,
      the real Mike,
      the Mike who always made me smile,
      the Mike who I knew was still there somewhere,
      could that Mike possibly, hopefully
be coming back to me?

INCOMING TEXT

Mary—
    can you sneak out?
Me—
    y?
Mary—
    party w Sam :)
    u in?
Me—
    yes!

SNEAK OUT

First,
a quick check
down the hall.

Mom and Dad's light?
      Out.
Mom and Dad's voices?
      Silent.

Will?
      Whatever.

I snick my door shut,
climb on the window sill,
and breathe.

Odds of getting caught?
      Small.
Worth it?
      Yes.

OW

I open the window,
grab the gutter,
squeeze my legs,
and slide
          down
                    dow-
                    ow
                         ow
                              ow
                                   down.

YOU DID IT?

"You did it!" Mary squeak-giggles.
       "We
weren't sure
       you
would dare."

"Why not?"
I try not
to look back,
but can't help a quick peek
at the shifting shadows
surrounding the dark windows
of the house I just left behind.
"We should go fast—
before someone wakes up.
If I get caught,
I'm dead."

"No worries."
Sam reaches back,
puppy pats my head.
"You're safe with me."

Sam slides the car down the road
as I grit-tooth smile and
       ignore the panic and
       ignore the worry and
       ignore the gutter-burn
screaming between my legs.

ON THE ROAD

Mary tells Sam where to go
on the sand-black back roads,
up the peninsula on the north side of the lake
where the houses get bigger
and the yards get wider
and the fences get higher and whiter.

My pulse does a stutter
as I wonder
how long we'll stay
and what Daddy might say
if he wakes up before I get home.

But I don't ask,
I don't speak,
I just let Mary talk-giggle-talk
on and on.

RED CUPS

Sam pulls me from the car,
      soft squeezes
my sweaty hand.
      "Don't worry about
being out.
      Your Dad will never know."

"She'll be fine—c'mon—let's get in line!"
      Mary grabs Sam's arm,
leads the way
      to the keg where they
fill red plastic cups
      like they know what they're doing.

I try to keep up,
      but get caught in a flood
of stale-sweat smelling
      bumping dancing strangers.

Someone is singing
      along with Dr. Dre,
someone else is shouting while
      a group of girl gigglers are sloshing and
a gaggle of guys are guzzling.

Warm beer is splashing,
      skunky brown liquid flowing.

Someone is shoving
      an overflowing red cup at me.

WHY NOT?

Mike might think
      I'm too young,
And Sam might think
      I'm too scared,
But they're both wrong.

I take the cup.
      I sip,
I gulp,
      I swallow.

I sip and swallow and gulp,
      and it's not until
I slurp only air,
      that I realize my red cup
is empty.

And I'm still
      thirsty.

FLIRT

By the third refill,
the flat brown slop smells delicious.

By the fourth one,
I'm thinking it's also nutritious.

By the fifth,
I'm a superstar.

I'm laughing,
hip-bumping,
teasing, tugging, twirling,
while boys are swirling,
whirlpooling
around me.

I'm clever,
I'm witty,
I'm sexy,
I'm a temptress.

I've got my arm around
the waist of a boy I don't know.
He's got his hand on my butt.

"What's your number?"

"I don't remember!"

I grab my cell
but he pushes it back,
shakes his head.

"Your sail, not your cell."
His voice tickles my ear.

I hiccup.
I laugh.
I cover my mouth and burp.

HAVE YOU SEEN SAM?

"Have you seen Sam?"

My beery question
makes butt boy
stop squeezing.

At the keg,
I hip bump Sam's thigh.

"I found you!"

My bump-shout makes Sam laugh,
and his laugh makes me laugh,
and then we're laughing together.

DRINKING GAMES

When I burp again,
Sam's grin sinks
into a Dad-sized frown.

"Are you OK?"

"I'm fine,"
I slur into his shoulder.
"I'm having fun—aren't you?"

"Danielle, I don't know,
maybe we should go . . ."

"S'ok, Sam, don't worry,
it's not like I'm just
some wimpy little kid—
        or scared—
or anything like that—
I do stuff like this
all the time."

I cross my fingers
and my toes
and hope that God
will forgive me
that one little beery lie.

"Maybe we should find Mary."

I tuck my chin
into Sam's neck
and whisper,
"Maybe we should find
a bedroom instead."

OMG!

Did I just say that?

How many beers have I had?

UP

It feels so right,
when I clutch Sam's hand tight,
and we sneak off to the king-sized water bed.

We lock the door,
and we dive into the silk sheets,
and our bodies twist and swim on the bumpy waterbed waves.

BUT THEN

But then . . .

Sam's arms
are seaweed

      wrapping,
          winding,
               trapping,
          squeezing,
     suffocating.

Sam's legs
are dead oak logs,

Sam's chest
is a cement block,

Sam's body
is drowning me.

go!

at first i'm saying
yes yes yes

and sam's moaning
go go go

and sam's whisper-humming
you're so beautiful

but now he's moving
fast and faster
and the room is
spin-twirling
and my head is
tilt-a-whirling

the beer said
i was ready
but sam's body
is so heavy
and i don't know
what i'm doing

stop!

WHAT WAS I THINKING?

"I thought this was what you wanted."

I thought so too.

SPIRALING DOWN

I push
I gag
I stand
I stumble

    . . .

I'm going under
       trapped like Jonah
           in a sloshy
               churny
                    white whale belly

THE MORNING AFTER

The next thing I remember
is the wind as it whacks
brittle branches against my window
that slap tap snap
me awake.

"No."
I moan and pull
Little Mermaid sheets
over my head.

It's too windy
it's too early
and I'm too sore
to sail.

EVERYTHING HURTS

Fire knives
slicing

Dull throbs
crashing

Pain
Ache
Burn

Head
Stomach
Arms
Legs
Fingers
Toes

Ego

Everything hurts.

DID I REALLY DO WHAT I HOPE I DIDN'T DO LAST NIGHT?

Pictures swim
across my mind like
technicolor fish trapped
in a ten-gallon tank—

      red cups
      buttery sheets
      shaggy carpet
      popped buttons
      sweat-wet t-shirt
      tangled matted bedhead

blue-eyed,
brown-haired,
buff-chested Sam -

and me.

what i remember

i can remember
the whoosh of cold air
where sam's hand used to be
when i leaned into the bushes
and puked.

the taste of bile
as i wiped my mouth
and slurred,
"where's mary?"

sam's trapped look
as his words swam
in the muck-thick dark night.
"mary's gone."

sam's car,
sam's pat,
sam's slide,
into the shadows of my front door

i can remember those things,
but then what?

did he leave me at the door?
how did i get inside?
upstairs?
in bed?
why do i think i remember

mike?

texting mary

me—
>*what happened last night?*

mary—
>*you get busted?*

me—
>*not yet—where were u?*

mary—
>*found a cute boy while u were w sam*

me—
>*i can't remember anything!*

mary—
>*want me to ask sam?*

me—
>*no!!!*

mary—
>*gotta go get ready*
>*gonna beat sam today*
>*and you and will 2*

GOD HELP ME

I have to crew for Will,

I have to see Sam,

I have to throw up.

BATHROOM BLITZ

I'm on my knees,
        head hanging over
        the Lysoled blue water,
trying to get rid of
        the evil,
        the pain,
the rolling,
        churning,
        acid burning
in my belly,
when a corps of
a thousand bass drums,
        timpani, snares, tom toms
        and woodblocks attack
the bathroom door.

Bang, kaboom, thud.

"Dani? Are you sick?"
Mom's shout is louder
than the loudest loud knock.
"Dani? Danielle?
Sweetie? Answer me! Are you OK in there?"

"I'm fine, Mom, fine, just fine, I swear."
But my reassuring shout
shoots deep into the porcelain bowl
and distorts in a squish
of wet echoes.

Mom makes a strangled sound
as her words come too high,
too fast.
"Brush your teeth,
wash your face
and get downstairs
before your father comes up."

What does she know?

FACE TIME

Spatula in hand
about to flip a pancake,
Mom pauses as I stand
blinking in the glare of
the too-bright yellow flowery kitchen.

"Pancake?" she asks.

I'm afraid I'll hurl
if I open my mouth,
so I shake my head instead.

Her face is lemon puckering,
her nose is pug dog wrinkling,
as she sniffs the fogging air.
"What's that smell?"

Resisting the urge
to run back to the bathroom.
I point to the smoking
charred pancake-shaped lumps
in the now blackened frying pan.

"Oh, dear."
Mom flips the charred remains
and sadly stares at the mess.
"What a waste."

GET IN, GET OUT

"Burning breakfast in here?"
        Daddy bops into the kitchen,
        grabs a coffee cup,
        pulls me down to the table beside him.
"Young lady, we need to talk."

Oh no—what does he know?

"It's supposed to blow
like everything today,
and I'm on call so I don't know
if I'll be able to be on the water."
        Daddy wipes black coffee
        off the edges of his mustache.

"But you need to know that you'll be fine.
The race committee will be watching—
they'll be keeping an eye on you—
and I promise,
you'll be fine,
as long as you stay calm."
        Daddy shoots one eyebrow up
        as he glub-glub drains
        his coffee cup and bangs
        it down on the table.

Ow.

Mom plops a bowl
of mushy grey oatmeal
in front of me.
"It's not pancakes or waffles,
but it's brown sugared up."

Daddy's voice rumbles on through the
rattle haze
of tidal-pain waves
crashing from my ears
to my gut
and down,
      down,
           to my toes.

"Just remember,
hang on, be strong,
be positive, be a good crew for your brother
and you'll be fine.
You'll see.
You will."

I stir-poke
the oatmeal mush
in front of me.

"Dani—Did you hear me?"

    Stir.
    Poke.
    Repeat.

        "Hang on. Be strong. Good crew. Will. Got it."

"Remember our deal,"
    Dad rumbles on.
"Stay tough, stay positive, win.
Sail smart; keep the piano."

        "Stay. Stay. Win. Smart. Piano. OK."

"You can do this, Danielle.
I know you can."

DON'T BE AFRAID

"Don't be afraid."
Daddy messes up my hair.
"You'll be OK.
Will can handle
a little wind.
You just be sure
to be calm
and hang on.
You'll be fine.
You'll see.

Remember,
you're a Biddle—
you were born to sail."

I push away
the oatmeal slop,
slap a smile on my face,
and slide to the door.
"I'll do my best."

"I know you will."

When Daddy says that,
it almost sort of,
possibly kind of,
sounds like he might be
potentially worried about me.

Then again
it could just be
echoes from the pounding
in my poor aching throbbing head.

HURRY

Out the front door
through the yard
rush rush run
don't slow, don't stop
not even for Mike—
Old or New.

I'M NOT FAST ENOUGH

Mike's voice catches me
before I get to the dock.

"DD—c'mon,
wait—
stop."

It sounds so much like
      Old Mike
that I can't help it—
      I stop.

"What?" I hold my head
and squint through the sun
at the stubby splotches
of new hair sticking
up all over his bad buzz cut.

ARE YOU OK?

"Are you OK?"
Mike almost looks me
in the eye
as he winds
a grease-spattered rag
through the stained fingers of one hand,
and spins a wrench in the other.
"Did you get in trouble last night?"

       I watch his wrench hand, sputter, stammer,
       "No—yes—I'm fine—why?"

Mike whacks his wrench
against a hunk of grease stained metal.
"You were pretty wasted."

       "How do you know?"

"Sailor boy was gonna bang the door and leave you."
The wrench stops, Mike looks up.
"I took care of him."

       I take a step back.
       I know that look.
       I whisper,
       "What did you do?"

"Whaddaya think I did? Got rid of him."

       "What did you do?"

"Brought you in."
Mike starts clanking
on the pieces of engine again.

       Mike's stone eyes smash into mine
       but it's too late—
       I can't blink back
       the words that splash
       out of my traitorous mouth.
       "What did you do to Sam?"

New Mike knifes his wrench
into the toolbox,
slams the lid.
"I didn't touch him.
And yeah, by the way,
you're welcome."

I'M SORRY!

Shouts
don't bring him back.

Begging
won't make him understand.

Talking
can't make him comprehend

that I don't really think
he'd really truly do
anything bad—
even after
Juvie.

JUVIE HAIKU

Mike went to Juvie
for stealing a car. His mom's
new boyfriend's Honda.

Boyfriend called the cops.
Mike resisted. Good-bye, Old
Mike. Hello, Juvie.

SPINNING

Stumbling
to the dock,
    tears
        splashing,
            vision
        blurring,
thoughts
    spinning,
        stomach
            churning,
                pain
            throbbing,
        manic
    cacophony,
chaotic
    symphony,
        flashing
            lights
                peppering,
            dragging,
        jerk-yanking,
images spinning inside me.

Sam,
    Old Mike,
        New.
                Wrenches,
        Waterbeds,
    red plastic
cups.

Tasting
    stale beer,
        aching
            everywhere.
    In the boat
    someone is talking—
Will?

LETTING WILL DRIVE

"This is so sweet—
thanks for letting me drive!"
Will revs the blue motor,
the tin boat jumps,
      I bounce and gag.
"Waves are huge today."

I can't answer,
      I'm leaning
            over the edge,
      ready to hurl,
not looking back but still seeing,
knife-pointed
white waves aiming
right for us.

"Awesome, right?
We're gonna fly
in this wind today."

                    He's just like Dad,
               they think water's fun
                 and wind is good
                   but they forget
                that wind destroys
               and water drowns.

CRASH LANDING

The bow of the tin boat
       is already dented
from Will ramming it into
       the dock.

Maybe that's why
       Dad says Will's not
supposed to
       drive.

But my head's spinning
       and I'm not trying
to stop him from doing it
       again.

Ouch.

I slip-slide down,
       off my seat,
we hit the dock hard,
       I see feet.

"Dani?"

       Sam.

WHAT DO I DO NOW?

Sam reaches down,
pulls me up,
without asking if I need help.
"Are you OK?"
He's smiling,
but I'm shivering,
and my cheeks are burning.

"Hi—" I try,

but Sam's already
dropped my hand,
turning to Will, saying,
"There's donuts
up at the Sailor's House."

"Let's go!" Will ties up,
takes off,
leaves me
all alone.

> *I wish Bessie were here*
> *I wish I could play this feeling away*
> *I wish I could I slip off,*
> *escape to a place*
> *where there is no wind*
> *there is no water*
> *there is no fear.*

If I could just play
then everything would slide
            back into place
                        like a thousand shreds
                                    from a ripped-apart love letter
windswept back together.

If I could just play
black water waves
of worry and doubt would fade
            into shallow blue ripples.

BLACK COFFEE

"Did you talk to him?"
Mary grabs me,
pulls me down the dock
towards her boat.
"What did he say?
Are you going to see him again?"

"I don't know."
I wrap an arm
around my crying gut,
and wonder if I'll ever
feel normal again.
"I gotta sit down."

When Mary shakes her head
her red hair burns in the sun
too bright, too bright.

She pushes an almost empty
lukewarm styrofoam cup
in my cold hands.
"Drink this—
it'll help."

The burnt tar smell
floating up from the black dregs
makes me gag.

RACE PREP RIGGING

Mary feeds
the rip-sharp edge
of her bright white mainsail
into the glinting groove on her boom.

I blink spots
out of my eyes
and see Will at the Sailor's House
talking to a vaguely familiar guy.

Somewhere deep
in my faulty foggy memory,
I seem to remember
a butt squeeze.

The guy is talking
to Will and looking
down the dock straight
at me.

Mary must
be watching them too.
"Does Will know what happened
last night?"

I'd shake my head no
if I weren't afraid
that the shaking
might make it
          explode.

DELICIOUS DONUTS

Sam passing out donuts
    when Will stomps up,
        his hands full of smushed
            chocolate-vanilla-sprinkle-frosted blobs.
Donut crumbs
    splatter and spew
        like a mad dash of plankton
           escaping the clutches
               of Will's wide-hinging killer-whale jaw,
but crumbs can't stop Will's spouting and shouting
    as he goes off at Sam,
        his food-filled voice louder
           than a foghorn.
"What did you do to her?"
    Will's fists are fisted,
        Will's face is twisted,
           I've never seen him this mad.
He's never stuck up
    for me before,
        but now he's shouting
           and spewing more crumbs
             across the gathering crowd.
"Will!" I tug-beg, trying to pull him back.
    "Be quiet, please,
        people are starting to stare."
The sweat on my face feels
    like boiling water,
        the rumbling in my stomach
           a waking volcano.
Will jabs a thick finger
    at Sam's sunburned nose.
        "Leave my sister alone."
"Sam didn't do anything,"
    I whisper-whisper-faster-faster.
        "It was me—
           it was those red plastic cups."
Smiling Sam pushes
    Will's finger away.
        "Don't worry, kid," Sam says, still grinning.
        "Your sister just wants
           to be friends. Right, Dani?"

MORE OR LESS

Yesterday—

I thought I wanted
to be more than friends,
I thought I wanted
Sam.

Today—

I know I don't want
that,
I just want
to win.

GOOD LUCK

Sam pats my silent head,
      shines his smile at the crowd,
and straightlines down
      the dock.

Over his shoulder,
      Sam calls back to us,
"Good luck today, kids,
      you're going to need it."

THE BEST MAN

"That guy's a jerk."
Will looks towards me
but not at me
focused on something
over my head.
"You OK?
You gonna be able to sail today?
You sure you're ready to go?"

      Flips and blips skip
      deep in my gut
      at the sight of Will's twitching
      tight fists.
      "Fine. Yes. Ready.
      Let's go."

PREP GUN

"Good luck, everyone!"
Mary shouts as we all push off
headed from the dock to
the starting line.

The wind is whooshing,
the waves are cresting,
the prep gun goes off,
the countdown begins.

"Ten minutes," I tell Will.

"Wind's picking up."
Will tightens a line.
"Get ready to hike—
hold on."

READY

Holding on,
lifejacket zipped,
jib tight,
toes tucked under
      wet hiking straps,
fingers
      curled
            around
the edge of the boat—

      Bring it on, wind.

STARTING LINE

Banging bumping
X boats clumping
waiting for the gun to blast.

"Starboard!" "Take it up!"
"Watch that boom, jackass!"
"Watch your mouth, Sam!"

I can't look
at the mosh pit of sailors
surging up like fans
at a rock show,
threatening to crash the stage,
      the race course,
and looking like they're going to smash
each other into driftwood.

I watch my watch
call out the minutes,
      the seconds,
           the count down,

3 . . .
     2 . . .
         1 . . .

GO!

Port tack
     the entire
fleet.

Cut across
     to the far side
of the course.

Round
     the first buoy
in first.

Round the
     low mark
in first.

Round and round
     and up
and down.

Always in
     the same order:
Will, Sam, Mary.

BATTLE

Fighting the wind,
  and the waves,
    and each other.

Mouths
  trash talk yapping,
Water
  cold slap dashing,
Sails
  angry bird flapping.

Faster,
  colder,
    louder.

MAJOR CHORDS

Stacked three deep,
the leaders lead.

      Will,
      Sam,
      Mary.

But we're the only three
      stable chords that are turning into a
            quickly decomposing composition.

The rest of the X boat
      fleet behind us
            are quickly losing control.

Boats are tip-flipping,
      kids are splash crashing,
            the lake is littered with upside down hulls
                  and swimming shouting sailors.

All the rescue boats
      are scrambling to pick up
            the pieces and pluck
                  waterlogged bodies out of the waves.

Dear God,
watch over us—
if we tip over
who will save us?

STOP LOOKING BACK

Will is standing,
shouting,
pointing in front of us,
making me tear my eyes away
from the disaster behind.

I'm wondering
why he's pointing
when the wind comes blasting
and we're flying,
and I'm screaming
and the boat is hydroplaning.

We're hit

                by a gust

and the boom

                          CRACKS

                across the deck

and I duck—

                but Will doesn't.

WILL!

With a dull skull thud,
Will's head snaps,
and his back arcs,
and his legs flop,
and his body drops
off the boat.

CAUGHT IN A WILLIWAW

Will's lifejacket

keeps hims

on the surface,

but he's face down

as he floats away

on whitecapping waves.

The wind

swoops back,

the boat jerks tilts

high in the air,

throws me out,

slams me down,

slaps her death white enormous sail

over me.

TRAPPED

My lifejacket can't
do her job,
can't keep me on
the surface
as the huge main sail
shoves me down,
down,
down.

I fight,
I kick,
I claw,
no luck.

Can't see,
can't breathe,
can't believe
this is happening again.

No.

This time
won't be like
the last time.

This time
I won't let
the sail keep me down.

This time
I've got to get

Will.

DIVE DEEP

White sail, white sail,
everywhichway up is white sail.

Need to dive deep,
for me, for Will.

Unclick lifejacket,
drop, shove, kick, swim.

Pull,
pull,
search—

    Which way is up?

No air,
no sound,
no more sense of direction -

    Have to find the up, have to get Will.

Burning lungs
pounding ears,
suffocating heart—

    Is Will still floating face down?

UNDERWATER

Green-black-blue
Silence
Cold liquid
Cemetery

ON THE DOWNBEAT

Screaming silence

Silence + underwater = panic attack freak out

Time for a new equation.

Thudding, crashing,
heartbeat smashing,
louder, closer, faster.

Hangover-head rattle-pounding—
      snare drums,
      bass drums,
      drum corps,
burning flashing hallucinations—
      plumed hats,
      marching band,
      green field,
      green murk,
silent directions sternly running—
      kick,
      pull,
      up you go,
      don't open your mouth,
      don't drink the water.

YES!

Still kicking
in time to the marching
band blasting in my head,
I break the surface
and see red.

Will's lifejacket is bright
in the white capping waves,
easy to find,
hard to reach.

I pull, kick, claw, stroke,
drag through syrup-thick waves.

Finally, finally, I'm here and he's there.

I grab, he flops,
his eyes are shuttered,
his face cadaver pale.

I hook an arm
under his neck,
swim for the upside down
close but far sailboat.

Kick, pull, drag, pray.

A PRAYER FOR WILL

Let him live
Let him be OK
Let this not be
his very last race

FINISH LINE

Spitting out water,
hanging onto Will,
hoping, praying, pinching, poking.

"Wake up, Will, wake up!"

He sputter spit sneezes,
rolls wild eyes right past me
to the upside down X boat
crashing in the cresting waves.

"What happened?"

"You fell out."

"You saved me?"

"Yes."

BEST HANGOVER CURE EVER

Maybe it's being
a savior for a brother
who normally never
needs saving,

or maybe it's practically drowning
in a wicked blast
of cold air and silent green-blue-black water,

but for whatever reason,
my head isn't thudding,
my gut's not tilt-a-whirling,
and even though I'm still stuck in the lake,

I feel great.

MARY

"Is everyone OK?"

I spin to see
my best friend Mary
has sailed herself
out of the race,
sailed her boat back
to us.

"C'mon," Mary leans over
and reaches for me and Will.
"I'll give you a ride
back to the dock."

"What about the race?"

Mary shrugs.
"Sam's probably won by now.
When he saw you flip,
he took off fast."

In the echo of her words,
we hear the gun
that signals the race winner
has crossed the line.

We look,
we see,
it's Sam.

THE BODEANS HAD IT RIGHT

"He's just another stupid boy,"
I sing soft and low
as Sam lands at the dock
right behind us.

> *I should have known*
> *he'd be*
> *just another stupid*
> *sailor boy.*

He was one
of the only ones left
mast up on a race course
staccato-dotted with capsized disasters.

> *I should have known*
> *he wouldn't be*
> *there for me*
> *when I needed him.*

Stupid boy,
selfish sailor,
forget him,
for now and forever.

I turn away
from stupid Sam,
shiver-watch other boats
get drag-towed in.

Waterlogged hulls spit out
shivering sailors with
blueing lips,
purpling skin.

BIDDLE CREED TAKE TWO

"William! Danielle!"

Daddy is running
     up the dock,
     scrubs rumpled, hair crumpled
     like he's been rubbing his head again.
Daddy is grabbing
     us and hugging,
     squeezing so tight
     I can't breathe.
Daddy is laughing and growling and demanding.
     "Are you OK?
     What happened? Where's the boat?
     What's wrong with Will? Tell me everything."

Mom is a half hug behind him.
     "Oh, sweeties,
     we were so worried."

She swans her long arms
around all three of us,
and we do a four person
family sing-sway.

     A Biddle's a sailor,
     A Biddle is strong,
     The first Biddles were whalers,
     and this is their song.

Mom hums, Daddy sings
and even though he's hardly standing,
Will joins in as well.

I'm the only one
not singing.

CUT

I step out of the family hug,
the family tears,
the family song.

I make the music
screech stop still
with two magic words—

    "Not me."

My announcement hits
like a surprise cymbal crash,
stunning into silence
the three-part Biddle band.

       I fill the silence stupidly.
          "I'm not a Biddle—
               I mean, I am a Biddle,
                   but I'm not a sailor,
                     not anymore,
                         not now that the regatta is over.
                         That was the deal,
                           right, Daddy?"

EXPECTATIONS

I expect:
> denial,
> argument,
> new deal making.

I get:
> nodding,
> chin rubbing,
> slow humming
>> of the Biddle tune.

Daddy shakes his head and stops the music.

"Someday,"
> Daddy hesitates, starts again.
"Someday you might want to sail again.
And you always can.
After all, you're a Biddle,
through and through."

"I can still be a Biddle
> at the keys of the piano."

Daddy takes a deep breath.
> "True.
> A deal is
> a deal.
> You can keep
> your piano."

I poof out the breath
> I didn't realize I'd been holding
and quick hug Daddy.

Holding Will with one arm,
Mom squeezes Daddy and me with the other,
and we're all together
in a family group hug again.

I'm caught in the middle,
but this time, I don't mind—

I bounce and sing
a mash up tune
of sailing Biddles and
safe pianos—

DANI'S SONG

Most Biddles are sailors
All Biddles are strong
One Biddle plays piano
And this is her song.

HOME

Mike's on the lawn when we motorboat in,
totally surrounded
by scattered pieces
of pulled-apart engine.

I go to him,
stand close but not too close,
whisper-sing soft,
"Mike, I'm sorry."

Old Mike looks up,
Old Mike's tools clink,
Old Mike nods and throws me a wrench.
"Wanna help?"

The wind swish-whispers
and my heart stutter flutters.

Trees and tools and heart harmonize,
mixing rhythm and melody,
a bittersweet blend of fear and hope,
the perfect mash up of possibility.

EPILOGUE

Dear Uncle Noah,

So there it is, my
long sob story in all it's
gory truth. Too much?

Hope not. Here's a last
long haiku for you. Give it
a back beat and go.

Once upon a time,
when I was just a little,
I couldn't say no.

Daddy told me what
to do. A Biddle always
sails. Daddy said so.

Maybe it was you
who finally changed Daddy's mind.
Your fall changed us all.

I know you don't want
sympathy, I know you don't
want poetry, but

this is the only
way for me to tell you that
I love you. You set

me free, got me off
the lake, gave me the chance to
play my piano

every day. I am
and I will. I'll play for you,
for me, for Daddy,

Mom and Will. I'll write
mash ups that sing our songs, ask
Mike to play along.

Keep getting better.
Keep driving your chair. I hope
I can see you soon.

Love,
Dani

About the Author

Anne Tews Schwab is a writer and a poet, a musician, music teacher and music therapist, a sailor, squash player, skier and biker. She loves writing, reading, music, carrots and waking up before the sun.

On any given day, Anne may be found filling the roles of novelist, poet, editor and teacher as well as doctor, lawyer, psychiatrist and chef. In other words, she is a writer, a wife and a mother of four. Anne lives in happy harmony with her husband, four children and one fluffy dog in a wooded house tucked between a large pond and a small lake.

Growing up in Minnesota, she developed her love of water before she was even able to walk. Anne explored area lakes and ponds by sailing and swimming through her childhood and teen years. Wind and waves remained essential elements in Anne's college years and beyond as she traveled the country and basked on the beaches of coastal rivers and oceans.

After graduating from Wellesley College with a BA in Psychology, Anne returned to the land of 10,000 lakes where she started a family, earned her MA in Music Education and Music Therapy from the University of Minnesota, ran a private music education and music therapy studio and earned her MFA in Creative Writing for Children and Young Adults from Hamline University.

Anne has published short stories and essays. She is currently working on an assortment of short stories, poetry and book reviews and navigating a final draft of her latest novel—a middle-grade fantasy adventure filled with pirates, plunder and plenty of plot twists.

Anne teaches classes for children and adults on creative writing, poetry, pirates and music.

Come and visit Anne on her website: www.piratepoems.com, where she posts a new pirate poem every day. You can also find Anne on Facebook: www.facebook.com/aschwabbie or www.facebook.com/PiratePoetryPlunder, and Twitter: https://twitter.com/aschwabbie or https://twitter.com/PoetryPlunder

Sing me a poem,
write me a rhyme. Story and
rhythm intertwine.

CAPSIZED Poetry in the Classroom
Music and Meter, Rhythm and Rhyme,
Writing Poem Songs like Dani

STEP 1:

What is a song? What is a poem?
Think about the relationship between those two things.

STEP 2:

Search for examples of song lyrics that tell a simple but gripping story.
Try searching through a variety of musical styles (past and present) to find different examples.
> Nursery rhymes
> Classic Rock / Popular Rock / Alternative Rock
> Country Western
> Rhythm and Blues / Jazz

Choose three specific songs and listen carefully.
Write out the lyrics of one verse plus the chorus from each song.

STEP 3:

Search the lyrics you wrote out in Step 2 to find poetic particulars.
Pay careful attention to examples of poetic devices such as:
> Alliteration—Using the same sound over and over again
> Rhyme—Using words that sound alike
> Onomatopoeia—A word that sounds like the word it represents, like "Boom!" or "Bang!"
> Personification - Giving human feelings to something that is not alive
> Metaphor - Comparing two things without using the words "like" or "as"
> Simile - Comparing two words using the words "like" or "as"

STEP 4:

Choose a topic for your poem / song. Brainstorm as a class or individually.
Here are some ideas to get you started...
> Underwater world
> Talking animals
> Hiding places
> Worst song
> Best book
> One word that changed an entire day
> Dancing into history
> Presidents, Queens and Kings
> High school / middle school / elementary school / preschool

Seasons
Allergies
Languages
Athletic flops
Spacecrafts and faraway planets
Outrageous headlines
Familiar smells
Surprising sounds

STEP 5:

Thinking about the poetic devices discovered and discussed in Step 3, choose at least three to use as you create a poem / song lyrics of your own.

Here are a few more ideas to get you started...
Couplet - a group of two lines that rhyme
Hyperbole - over exaggeration
Parody - imitating and making fun of something at the same time (a book, a painting, a nursery rhyme, a song)

STEP 6:

Choose a poetic style -- free verse or a fixed form.
Acrostic
Choose a one or two word topic.
Write the letters of the word vertically down the page.
Write each line horizontally using the letters in descending order.
Alphabet
Arrange the lines (or words) of the poem in alphabetical order (A to Z or Z to A).
Cento
Pick out lines from other people's poetry and put them together in your own way.
You can can add rhythm and rhyme by using the aa, bb, cc format.
aa = first two lines rhyme
bb = second two lines rhyme in a different way than the first two
cc = next two lines rhyme in a new way
Cinquain
A non-rhyming but rhythmic form.
Five lines with specific syllabic counts:
Line 1 = two syllables
Line 2 = four syllables
Line 3 = six syllables
Line 4 = eight syllables
Line 5 = two syllables.

Clerihew

A great form especially if you are stuck for a topic because the topic of this poem can be YOU!

This poetic form has four lines.

Line 1 = your name

Lines 2-4 = clues about you

This form also has a set rhyme pattern:

aa (Lines 1&2 rhyme)

bb (Lines 3&4 rhyme)

You can also use someone else's name for this poem, but be sure to ask them for permission first - some people prefer to remain anonymous.

Diamante (the form that Dani uses to describe a beautiful Steinway piano)

Seven lines of ascending and descending size.

When put together, words form the shape of a diamond.

Line 1 = one word (usually the topic)

Line 2 = two words (usually descriptions (adjectives) about the topic)

Line 3 = three words (usually verbs (action words) about the topic)

Line 4 = four words (either a four word phrase about the topic OR a twist where the first two words describe the topic and the next two words describe the opposite of the topic, leading to a completely different ending where the last lines would be about this opposite side of the topic)

Line 5 = three words (usually verbs (action words) about the topic or if using the twist, the opposite of the topic)

Line 6 = two words (usually descriptions (adjectives) about the topic or the twisted opposite side)

Line 7 = one word (topic or opposite of the topic)

Haiku

A simple poem with Japanese roots, originally created to be about nature, without simile or metaphor or complete sentences and based on the sounds of the Japanese words, not the syllabic counts.

However, for our uses here, we shall bow to the modified and simplified Americanized version where the subject is wide open, the use of poetic devices such as simile and metaphor are allowed and the lines are formed around syllabic count instead of sounds.

Our haiku form shall be three lines with the following structure:

Line 1 = five syllables

Line 2 = seven syllables

Line 3 = five syllables.

Sonnet

Hello, Mr. Shakespeare! This is the poetic form most people associate with William Shakespeare.

A fourteen line poem with ten syllables per line, divided into two general sections.

Section One is made up of three groups of four lines each.

Section Two is a final group of two lines that summarize the previous twelve.

The rhyme scheme is as follows:

> abab
> cdcd
> efef
> gg

STEP 7:

Write the poem!

STEP 8:

After completing your poem, go back to the three song choices from Step 2.
Set the words of your poem to the melody of one of your original choices.
If your words do not match any of your melodies, keep searching.
Nursery rhymes are often good choices for simple melodies.
If no melody seems to fit, create a simple and memorable melody of your own.

STEP 9:

After fitting your words to a melody or creating a melody of your own, teach your poem song to the rest of the class.

Explain what your subject means to you, what poetic devices you used, what form you used and how you chose your melody.

STEP 10:

Discuss what works well, what could be changed or edited, what was frustrating, what was simple, what was fun.

STEP 11:

Collect all poem songs (with melodic instructions) and print copies to pass out to every class participant.

STEP 12:

Sing!
As a class, sing all songs together and if possible, record for future listening fun.